1896

Can You Say Peace?

Karen Katz

SQUARE
FISH

Henry Holt and Company

New York

SQUARE FISH

An Imprint of Macmillan
175 Fifth Avenue
New York, NY 10010
mackids.com

Square Fish and the Square Fish logo are trademarks of Macmillan and
are used by Henry Holt and Company, LLC under license from Macmillan.

Our books may be purchased in bulk for promotional, educational, or business use.
Please contact your local bookseller or the Macmillan Corporate and Premium Sales Department
at (800) 221-7945 ext. 5442 or by e-mail at MacmillanSpecialMarkets@macmillan.com.

Library of Congress Cataloging-in-Publication Data
Katz, Karen.
Can You Say Peace? / Karen Katz
p.   cm.
Summary: Every September 21 on the International Day of Peace,
children around the world wish in many different languages for peace.
ISBN 978-1-250-07321-1 (paperback)
[1. International Day of Peace—Fiction. 2. Peace—Fiction.] I. Title.
PZ7.K15745Can 2006   [E]—dc22   2005012857

Originally published in the United States by Henry Holt and Company, LLC
First Square Fish Edition: 2016
Book designed by Laurent Linn
Square Fish logo designed by Filomena Tuosto

1 3 5 7 9 10 8 6 4 2

LEXILE: AD260L

To all the children around the world,
our peacemakers of the future

Thanks to Kate Farrell, Laurent Linn, and Elaine Schiebel

Special thanks to Janos Tisovszky
and everyone at the United Nations
who taught me so many different ways
to say peace

Today is Peace Day
all around the world.
Children everywhere will
wish for peace,
hope for peace,
and ask for peace.

All around the world today, there will be many different ways to say *peace*.

Meena lives in India.

Meena says *shanti* (SHAHN-tee).

Emily lives in America.

Emily says *peace.*

Kenji lives in Japan.

Kenji says *heiwa* (hey-wah).

Lynette lives in Australia.

Lynette says *kurtuku* (kur-TU-ku).

Carlos lives in Mexico.

Carlos says *paz* (pahs).

Hana lives in Iran.

Hana says *sohl* (sohl).

Stefan lives in Russia.

Stefan says *mir* (meer).

May lives in China.

May says *he ping* (hey ping).

Claire lives in France.

Claire says *paix* (pay).

Sadiki lives in Ghana.

Sadiki says *goom-jigi* (goom-jee-jee).

Alona lives in Bolivia.

Alona says *mojjsa kamaña* (moh-khsah ka-mah-neeah).

All around the world, children want to go to school,

to walk in their towns and cities,

to play outside,

and to share food with their families.

They want to do all these things and feel safe.
No matter how we say it, we all want peace.

Can you say peace?

shanti

paix

he ping

mir

The United Nations has declared September 21
International Day of Peace.
All around the world people observe a day of peace and nonviolence.
They may conduct ceremonies honoring peace, participate in community
projects, or take a moment to silently wish for peace for everyone.
On this day people everywhere can find their own way to celebrate peace.

United States
Peace (English)

France
Paix (French)

Russia
Mir (Russian)

China
He ping
(Mandarin)

Iran
Sohl (Farsi)

Japan
Heiwa (Japanese)

Mexico
Paz (Spanish)

Ghana
Goom-jigi (Buli)

India
Shanti (Hindi)

Bolivia
Mojjsa Kamaña
(Aymara)

Australia
Kurtuku (Warnman)

More Ways to Say Peace

Country	Language	Word for peace	Pronunciation
Denmark	Danish	*Fred*	frehd
Egypt	Arabic	*Salaam*	sa-LAHM
Germany	German	*Frieden*	FREE-den
Greece	Greek	*Irini*	eh-REE-nee
Hungary	Hungarian	*Béké*	BAI-keh
Iceland	Icelandic	*Friður*	fri-eer
Israel	Hebrew	*Shalom*	shah-LOHM
Italy	Italian	*Pace*	PAH-chey
Poland	Polish	*Pokój*	poh-KOY
Tibet	Tibetan	*Sidi*	SHEE-deh
Vietnam	Vietnamese	*Hòa Bình*	hwah bean